IDA MAKES A MOVIE

LIBRARY OF CONGRESS
CATALOGING IN PUBLICATION DATA
Chorao, Kay.
    Ida makes a movie.
    SUMMARY: Ida is troubled when the judges of the
Children's Film-Making Contest award her movie first
prize, but completely misinterpret the plot.
    I. Title.
PZ7.C4463Id   [Fic]   73-20147
ISBN 0-8164-3121-3

IDA MAKES A MOVIE

Story and Pictures by
KAY CHORAO

A Clarion Book
THE SEABURY PRESS · NEW YORK

I T WAS A heavy hot day. The sun glowed white like a slice of raw potato.

Ida sat on the curb and sang a little song,

"Chewing tar is fine with me
But Mama says it is fil-thy."

"Ida, did you spit out that tar?" called Ida's mama from a window up above.

"YES," yelled Ida, spitting out a wad.

She was mad at her mama for making her spit out the tar. She was mad at her friends for going away for the summer (all except Cookie Pickens, who was so young she hardly counted). And she was mad at herself for having nothing to do.

"Mom, I'm hungry," yelled Ida.

Then she remembered. She had a whole tray of root beer frozen into cubes in the refrigerator. Each cube had a toothpick in it.

So Ida ran into her building, rode up her elevator, and rushed into her kitchen to examine the sixteen tiny popsicles.

She ate three and put the others on a plate with a sign that read, "Popsicles Hommade 2¢."

"Maybe Cookie will buy one or two," said Ida, arranging them nicely on a plate with each cube sitting in a tiny brown puddle.

Then Ida put the plate on a stool, grabbed her brother Fred's binoculars, and left.

When Fred got back from a movie he found Ida peering through his binoculars. And he found Cookie Pickens sitting beside Ida, sucking a toothpick. And beside Cookie Pickens sat four dollies, all sucking toothpicks, too.

"Who gave you permission to use my binoculars?" said Fred.

"Mom," said Ida.

"They're all sticky!" said Fred, snatching them away from his sister.

"Anyway, I made 24¢ from Cookie," whispered Ida.

"Hey, look at that. Something about making *movies*," said Fred.

He watched a bus pass along the park. The bus stopped.

"Movie making contest for children to age 12. Send films to National Film Board, Box 8, by July 7," read Fred from a poster on the bus.

"Want to make a movie?" asked Ida.

"Me too," squealed Cookie.

"We'd never win a contest," said Fred. "Besides, we always fight over who's going to pose and who's going to shoot. And besides that, our movies are always disasters, especially the ones *you* make."

Then he turned away and went into the building.

But Ida had an idea.

The next morning Ida got out the movie camera. It was an old one that Daddy had left behind in a humidor, along with some socks that had needed darning for years and years.

Ida loaded the camera with color film, the way she had seen Fred do it.

Then she raced around the apartment gathering things like plastic flowers, aprons, and hats that were crumpled and dusty from being on the closet shelf. She jammed everything into a supermarket bag.

"I'm glad you've found something better to do than chew tar," Ida's mother said.

"I'm making a movie!"

"That's fine," said Ida's mother, watching Ida drag the supermarket bag out the front door.

"I'm stopping for Cookie Pickens on the way down," called Ida.

But when Ida got to Cookie's apartment, Cookie had left.

Ida found her on the sidewalk, licking a cherry ice. She had her dollies all lined up again, still sucking their toothpicks.

"I'm teacher. They're all bad, bad children. We're playing school," said Cookie.

"I'm shooting a picture. Want to be a movie star?" asked Ida.

"Yes, I'm good at that," said Cookie. She clamped her teeth into a smile.

"No, no. I mean *real* movies. Lights, camera, ACTION!" said Ida.

Cookie stared at Ida and let the last of her cherry ice drip down her pinafore.

"You're nuts," she said.

But Ida could see that she was impressed.

"I'm the director," said Ida. "You do what I tell you to do. O.K.?"

"O.K.," said Cookie.

"Don't expect to win any contests," Fred shouted, leaning out his window.

"Don't pay any attention to *him*," whispered Ida.

"Boys are bad," said Cookie.

Ida wrapped a huge apron around Cookie. Then she put a plastic flower in her hair.

"Now, when I yell ACTION, you dance," said Ida.

"Lights, camera, ACTION!"

Cookie twirled around, tripping now and again on the apron strings.

"You are a beautiful girl at a dance, but you were supposed to wear a white dress instead of a green one, so everyone is staring at you and saying, 'My she is beautiful, but so terrible for not wearing white!' "

"That's silly," said Cookie, still twirling.

"It's not. It's serious. I saw a movie just like it on TV," said Ida, dipping her camera to film the row of dolls with their toothpicks.

"They are the audience, watching," said Ida.

Then Ida stopped the camera and shoved an old straw hat with streamers on Cookie's head.

"Fred, I need you!" called Ida.

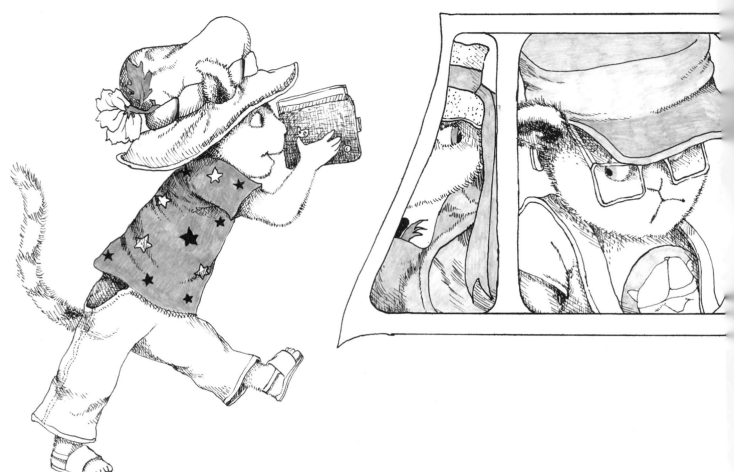

Fred poked his head out the window. Then after a few
moments he appeared on the sidewalk.

"This better not take long," he grumbled.

"You are Cookie's boy friend, see? And you don't like her
any more because she wore the green dress. So you are going
away forever. Cookie, you are mad at Fred."

Ida put an old Army hat on Fred.

"Lights, camera, ACTION!"

Cookie hit Fred in the stomach. Then Fred knocked her straw hat off. Then Cookie stuck her tongue out at Fred and started to cry.

"ENOUGH!" screamed Ida.

Up the street someone had opened a fire hydrant. A nice flow of water pushed its way down the street, carrying with it bits of paper and garbage. This gave Ida an idea. She reached into her prop bag and dug out a fistful of plastic flowers. These she stuck in Cookie's hair.

"Now, Cookie, everyone has gone away and left you and you are mad and crazy. Run up the street to the water."

Cookie staggered and stumbled up the street with the flowers hanging down from her hair.

"Good," Ida said, running after Cookie with the movie camera.

But then Cookie bumped into a sanitation man, who was feeding some bedsprings to a garbage truck.

Ida turned her camera onto the sanitation man, up his
uniform to his angry face, then down his arm to a bald dolly
he was now feeding into the truck.

"You're *mean!*" Cookie said, staring at the sanitation man.

But the garbage machine gobbled the dolly right up.

Then Ida remembered her job.

"Run into the water, then fall down and pretend to float away in the river," said Ida.

Cookie ran right into the spray. She giggled and rolled onto the street, dropping plastic flowers all over.

Ida turned her camera onto a plastic poppy traveling down the gutter like a little red boat. It floated right out of sight.

Then the film ran out.

"Bravo," said Ida. "We finished the movie!"

Fred snickered a little and walked away.

"I'm all wet and dirty," cried Cookie.

But Ida was pleased.

That night she sat down and wrote to the judges of the contest.

> "Be nice to Cookie and me
> Cause we worked as hard as a bee
> Fred says it's awful
> But he's an old waffle
> Sincerely yours, signed Idie."

The next day Ida had her film developed, and when it was ready she sent it off to the contest, along with the letter.

After that Ida spent quite a bit of time sitting on the curb, wondering if she would win the contest. There must be a prize. Maybe she would get a Rusty Rooter Pinball Machine. Or a remote-controlled airplane that buzzed overhead like a blender.

But two weeks later a package came from the contest center. There was a letter inside.

Dear Contestant,

We are sorry to inform you that you are not the lucky entrant. Your film is enclosed. Thank you for entering.

Sincerely,
HARRY DRUFFLE
Chairman

Ida was disappointed. She threw the movie into a drawer
and buried her head in a pillow to hide her tears.

"Fred is right. Everything I do is a disaster. Especially my movies," said Ida.

"No, dear, you mustn't feel that way," said Ida's mother, patting Ida's head gently.

"You freeze good root beer popsicles," said Fred, who was feeling a little guilty.

"I just can't do anything right," sighed Ida.

"If you really want to be a film maker, then get some books out of the library and read how to do it properly," said Ida's mother. "To start with, why don't we see the movie you made."

"She threw it in my underwear drawer," said Fred.

Ida rolled her eyes to the ceiling. "You see, I can't do *anything* right. I thought I put it in *my* drawer."

Fred fished the film out of his drawer and threaded it onto the projector. Ida got out the screen and Ida's mama pulled the shades.

The movie projector buzzed.

Onto the screen came a little girl, doing magic tricks with a top hat.

"That's not MY movie!" yelled Ida.

"That's not Cookie Pickens!" yelled Fred.

"That must be someone else's film," said their mother.

"Maybe they burned yours," said Fred.

Tears came to Ida's eyes and she ran out of the room. But Ida's mother went to the telephone.

She looked up the National Film Board in the telephone
directory and dialed the number.

Fred watched.

"There must be some mistake. Do you have my daughter's
movie?" said Mama.

Then Fred watched his mother nod and frown, with the
receiver to her ear.

"Hummmm. Yes. I see. No. Thank you, anyway," said
Mama.

And she hung up.

"I'm sorry, Ida," said her mother. "Harry Druffle says the only movie they have left is the winning one. It's something about war, and dolls with toothpicks, and flowers in the gutter."

"THAT'S IT!" yelled Ida and Fred together.

"That's it?" said their mother.

"That's really it," whispered Ida, hugging her doll, Clarence.

So Ida, herself, telephoned Harry Druffle and told him that the winning film was hers.

But she didn't tell him that he had the story all wrong.

As Ida's reward she was given a trip to the Magoona Beach Film Festival, which had a special section for children's films this year.

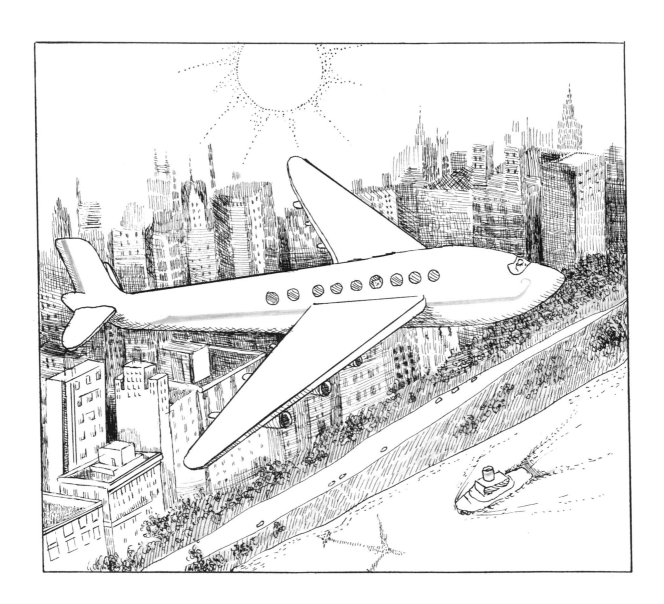

Harry Druffle and Ida's mother went along.

(Poor Fred had to stay with a neighbor, but she let him read her movie magazines and eat fudge between meals.)

Ida had never been on an airplane before, but Magoona Beach was on the ocean, far away. So she and Mama and Harry Druffle flew.

On the airplane they ate a meal served on a plastic tray with a lot of little holes for the food to sit in. Ida nibbled a mint that came in an envelope and she slipped a tiny salt shaker into her pocket.

But something was wrong. Ida felt a little sick, and it wasn't the airplane.

"Mama, my film wasn't about war at all," said Ida.

"I know," said Ida's mother.

"But that's wrong. It's like cheating, or telling a lie. I'm taking a prize for an idea I never had."

Ida felt she might cry. Right on her meringue glacé.

"Don't worry, dear," said Ida's mother. "Critics always have their own ways of seeing things, and it is best to let them think what they like. After all, I'm an artist. I should know."

Then Ida's mama kissed Ida's ear, and Ida slid down in her seat with her eyes closed.

When they landed, they went to a pink hotel with a swimming pool shaped like a bean.

The pool overlooked the ocean, which Ida said was silly. But she wore a bikini, and sipped mineral water, and watched the waves come in along the beach in long white rows. And she tried not to think about her movie. If she told the truth, would they boo and throw rocks?

That night Ida and her mother and Harry Druffle got all dressed up and went to the film festival.

Ida's dress prickled and she had to listen to a boring speech given by a man with blue chin whiskers.

"Mama, I'm scared," whispered Ida.

But then Mr. Druffle went to the stage and thanked everyone for making room in their evening for Ida's movie. He explained how Ida had used her own sidewalk and dolls and friends to show how terrible war is to little children.

When he sat down, Ida's movie was shown, and afterward everyone clapped hard, especially Mama.

Then Harry Druffle called Ida to the stage, and she felt sick again.

A big gold statue sat on a pillow. It was for her. But would they give it to her if she told the truth? Ida's heart pounded.

Harry Druffle pushed the statue under Ida's nose. His smile was so wide Ida counted three gold fillings. Ida felt terrible.

Ida's mother sat on the edge of her seat.

"I can't do anything right," whispered Ida into the microphone.

Harry Druffle's mouth fell right open.

"My movie wasn't supposed to be about war. It was supposed to be about a girl at a dance who wore a green dress instead of a white one. I saw the story on TV. My brother, Fred, made me watch it instead of Pearly Opossum's Neighborhood."

Ida stopped and looked at her feet.

A few people in the audience snickered.

Some tears rolled down Ida's nose and bounced onto her party shoes.

"Well, I never," said Harry Druffle.

"THREE CHEERS FOR A YOUNG LADY WHO KNOWS HOW TO TELL THE TRUTH!" bellowed the blue-whiskered man. Then he plucked a carnation from his buttonhole and gave it to Ida.

"Hip-hip HOORAY!" yelled the audience.

Then Ida skipped down the steps to Mama.

"I'm so proud of you, Ida," said Mama.

Harry Druffle stood speechless, holding the statue, but the man with whiskers grabbed the microphone.

"Come back, young lady. Your movie was judged the best, no matter *what* it was all about. This statue belongs to you!"

So Ida ran back and got her prize and thanked the man— and Harry Druffle.

Everyone clapped again when Ida left hugging the statue, and Ida's Mama left hugging Ida.

"My dress still prickles," whispered Ida.

But she stole a happy peek at her statue and whispered all to herself,

> "She is my golden lady
> I'll name her Delicious Sadie."

And she did.

DATE DUE			
FEB